**www.enchantedlion.com**

First English-language edition, published in 2022 by Enchanted Lion Books,
248 Creamer Street, Studio 4, Brooklyn, New York 11231



ISBN 978-1-59270-374-6


A CIP record is on file with the Library of Congress

Distributed by Consortium Book Sales & Distribution
Printed in Latvia by Livonia Print

First Printing

FSC www.fsc.org MIX Paper from responsible sources FSC® C002795

KJERSTI ANNESDATTER SKOMSVOLD
& MARI KANSTAD JOHNSEN

TRANSLATED FROM NORWEGIAN BY KARI DICKSON

# BEDTIME FOR BO

Enchanted Lion Books
NEW YORK

It’s evening and Bo is being silly.

He does tumblesaults on the sofa
and sings as loud as he can.

Mommy laughs.

"It's bedtime, Bo."

Bo stands on one leg. “I’m already asleep!”

“What do you mean?” asks Mommy.

“I’m a parrot,” says Bo.

"This is how a parrot sleeps,
like I'm standing now. On one leg."

"So it does!" says Mommy. "It tucks
one foot under its feathers, so it
won't get cold toes."

"Would my little parrot like something to eat?"

"Yes," says Bo,
flying into the kitchen.

He chirps away
about blueberries
and porridge.

"Your wish is my command!"
says Mommy.

“Do all animals have to sleep?” asks Bo.

“Yes,” says Mommy. “Even bees and wasps need to sleep. And cows do, too, but not as much.”

Bo yawns.

"I've eaten so many blueberries that I can sleep all winter long."

He hops down from his chair and crawls
under the table, into his cozy den.

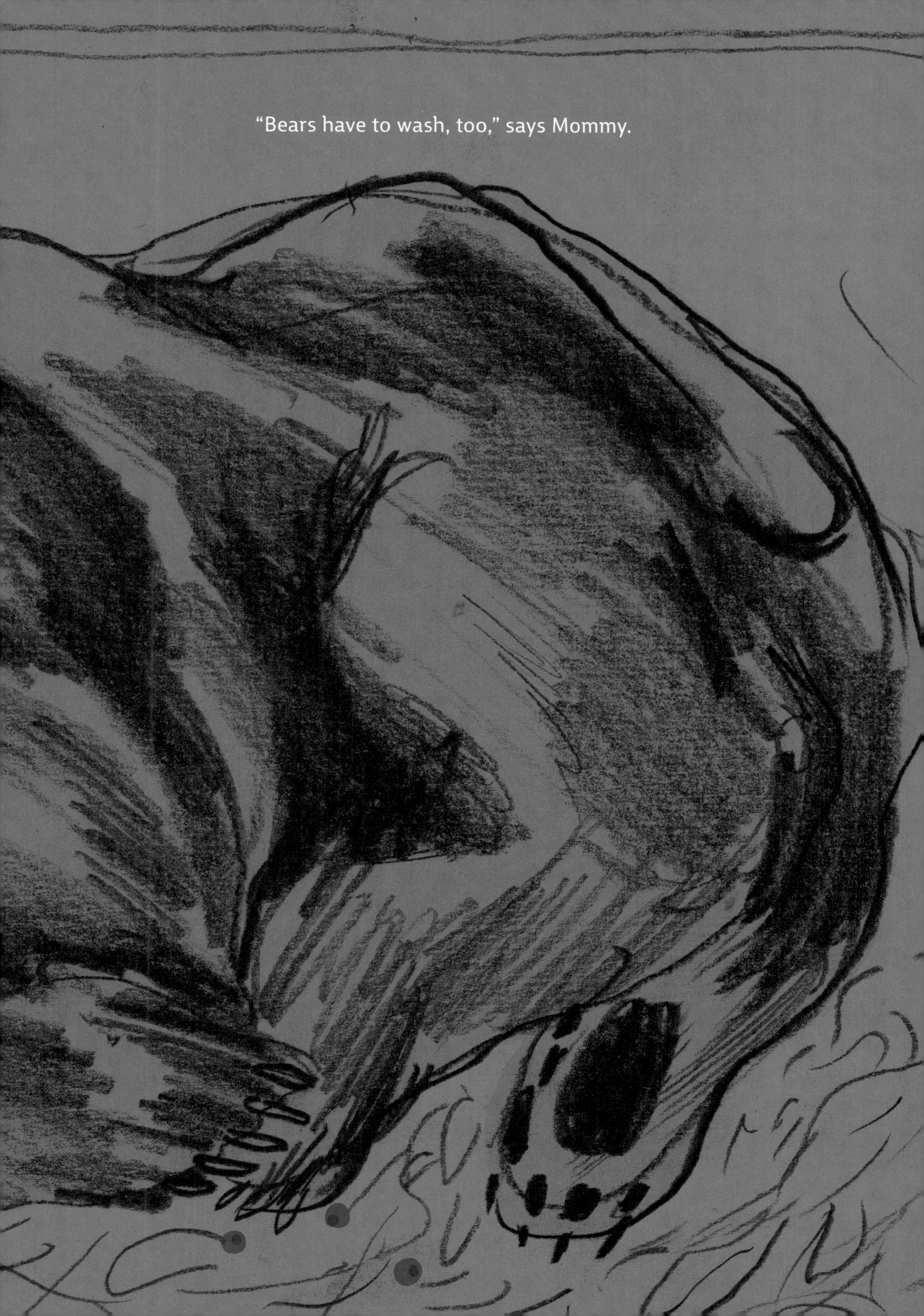

“Bears have to wash, too,” says Mommy.

Mommy turns on the faucets and
Bo climbs into the bathtub.

Soon, almost all of Bo is submerged
in warm water.

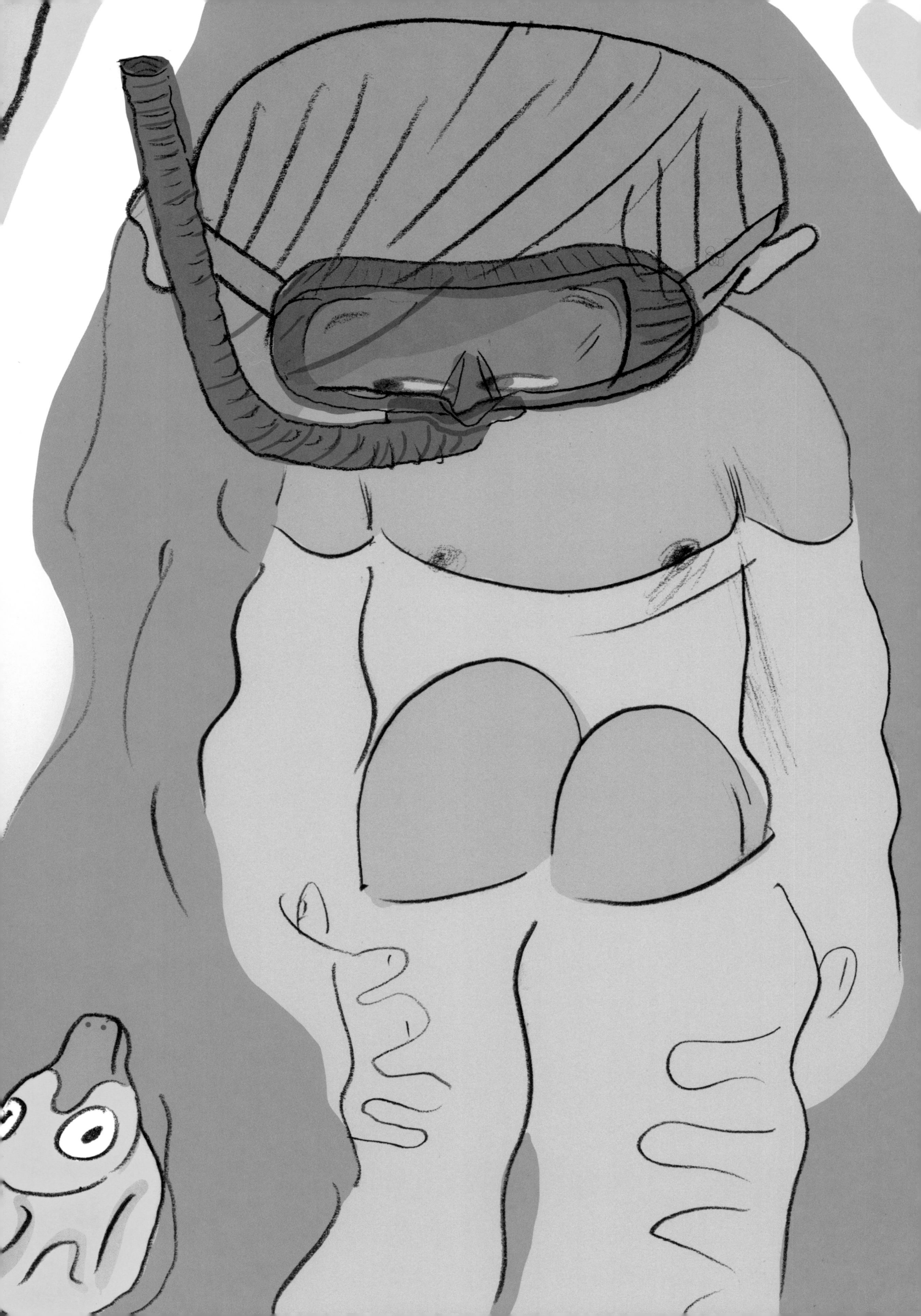

"I can't sleep here,"
says Bo. "What if I float away
and get lost in the ocean?"

"You can be a sea otter," says Mommy. "I'll wrap you in seaweed, and secure you like an anchor. I'll hold your hand in mine, so you won't disappear."

"Or perhaps a walrus?" continues Mommy. "You can hook your long tusks over the ice and hang on. Then you won't float away."

Bo bites the edge of the bathtub. "Like this?"

"Yes," says Mommy. "But those teeth need cleaning!"

Bo climbs out of the tub. His fingers are like raisins, and so are his toes. Mommy dries him off. Then, she brushes his teeth, top and bottom. When Bo is ready to spit into the sink, he has to stretch out his neck as far as he can.

"Now I'm a giraffe," says Bo. "Look at my neck!"

"Yes, a baby giraffe," says Mommy. "When you go to sleep, you curl your long neck back and rest your head on your bottom. It makes the perfect pillow."

"Mommy, look! There's a lion behind the toilet!" says Bo. "It's going to jump out and eat me up!"

"I'll protect you," says Mommy. "The giraffe mom sleeps on her feet, standing over her child like a watch tower."

With one eye open, Mommy stares sternly at the toilet.

“Oh no!” cries Mommy.
“The lion is coming for us.
Run, little one!”

They charge into the bedroom.

Bo pulls on his pajamas as fast as
he can, then wriggles under the bed.

“Lots of animals hide when they’re going to sleep,” says Mommy. “Some fish hide under sand and stones, and pandas and squirrels sleep in trees.”

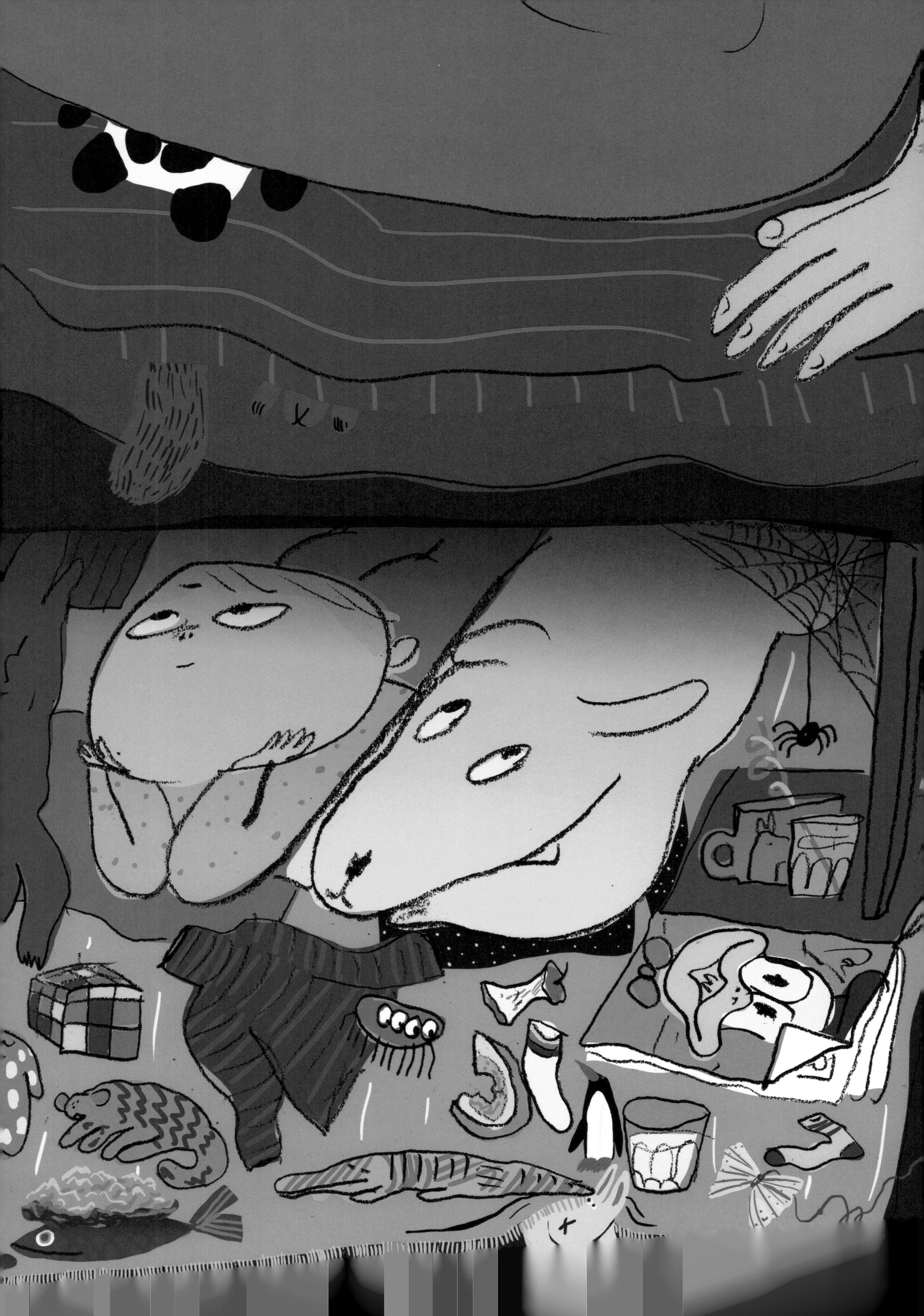

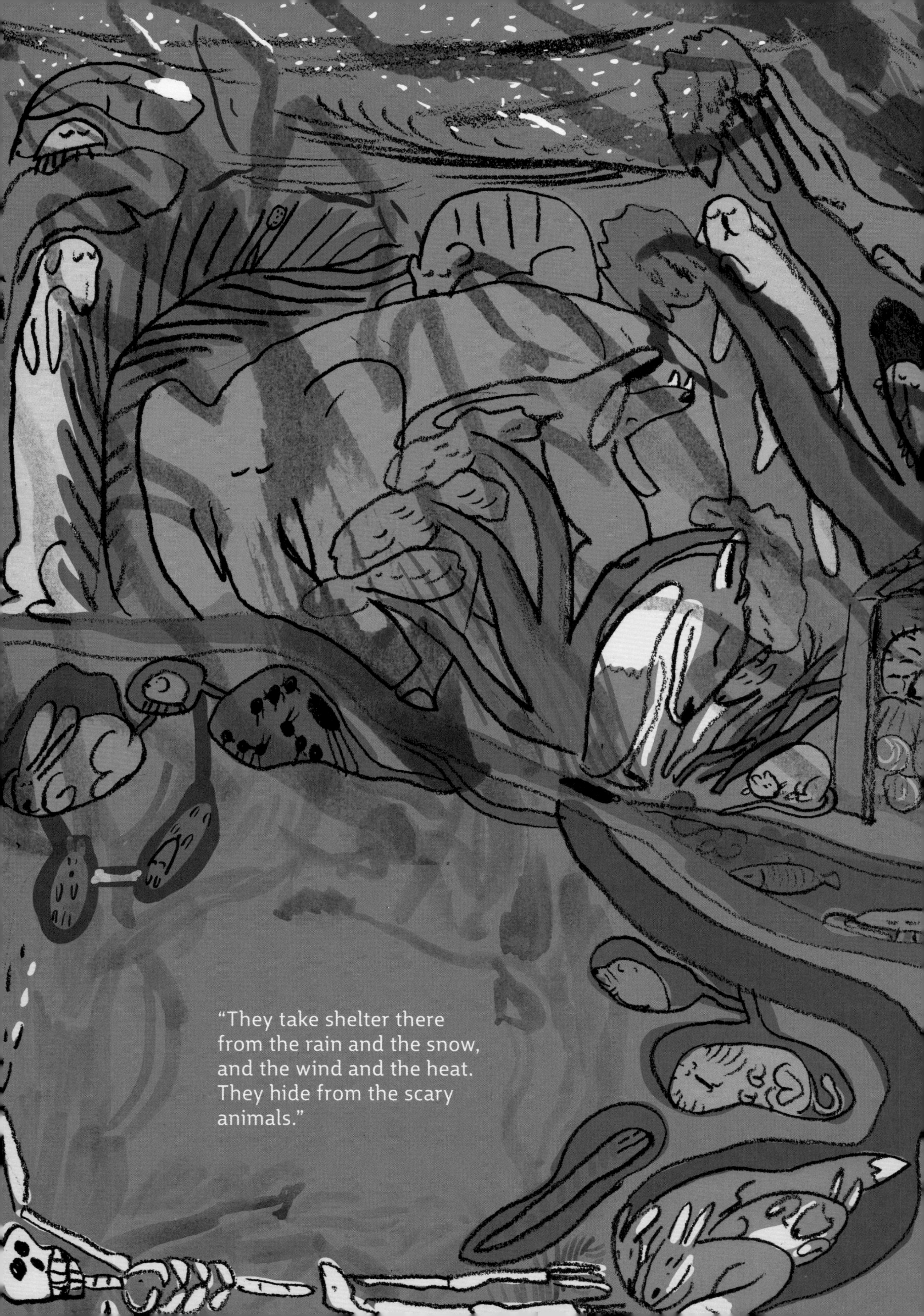

“They take shelter there
from the rain and the snow,
and the wind and the heat.
They hide from the scary
animals.”

Bo peeks out and crawls from under the bed.
With a pounce, he's standing on his head.

"Look at me!" says Bo. "I'm a bat!"

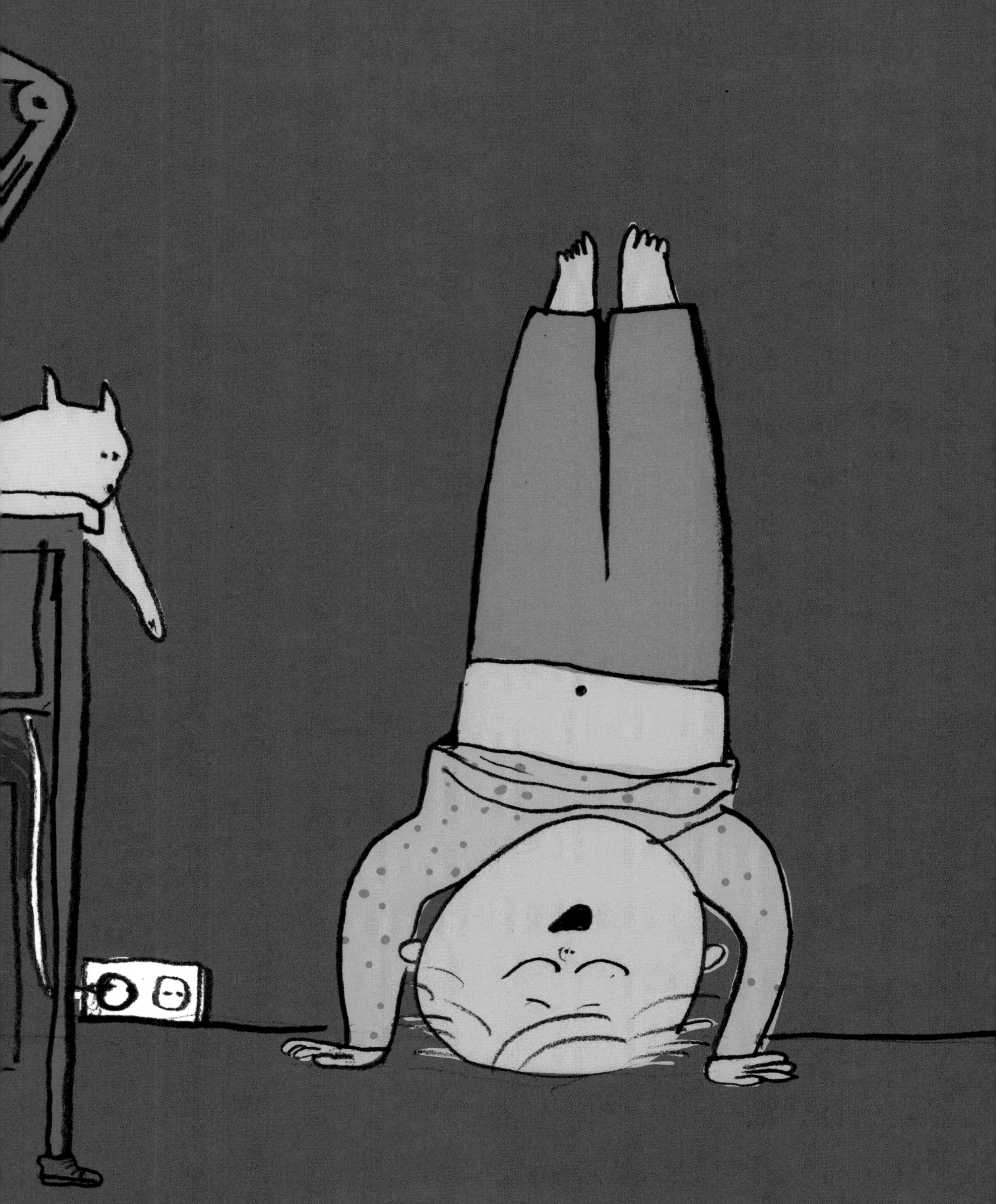

“Your wings are so heavy that you can’t leave the ground,” says Mommy. “If you hang from a big, old tree, you’ll find it easier to fly off.”

"And I won't have nightmares, either!" says Bo, his face bright red.

"What do you mean?" asks Mommy.

"The nightmares will run out of my ears," says Bo. "They'll disappear down into the grass."

But Bo can't stand on his head any longer.
He would rather sleep in his bed.

Laying his head on the pillow, he curls up
like a super long python.

Mommy tucks Bo in and strokes his hair.

"Now you're a mob of meerkats," says Mommy. "You sleep all snuggled up, over and under each other. That's how you keep yourselves warm."

Bo rubs his eyes and yawns again. He feels so tired.

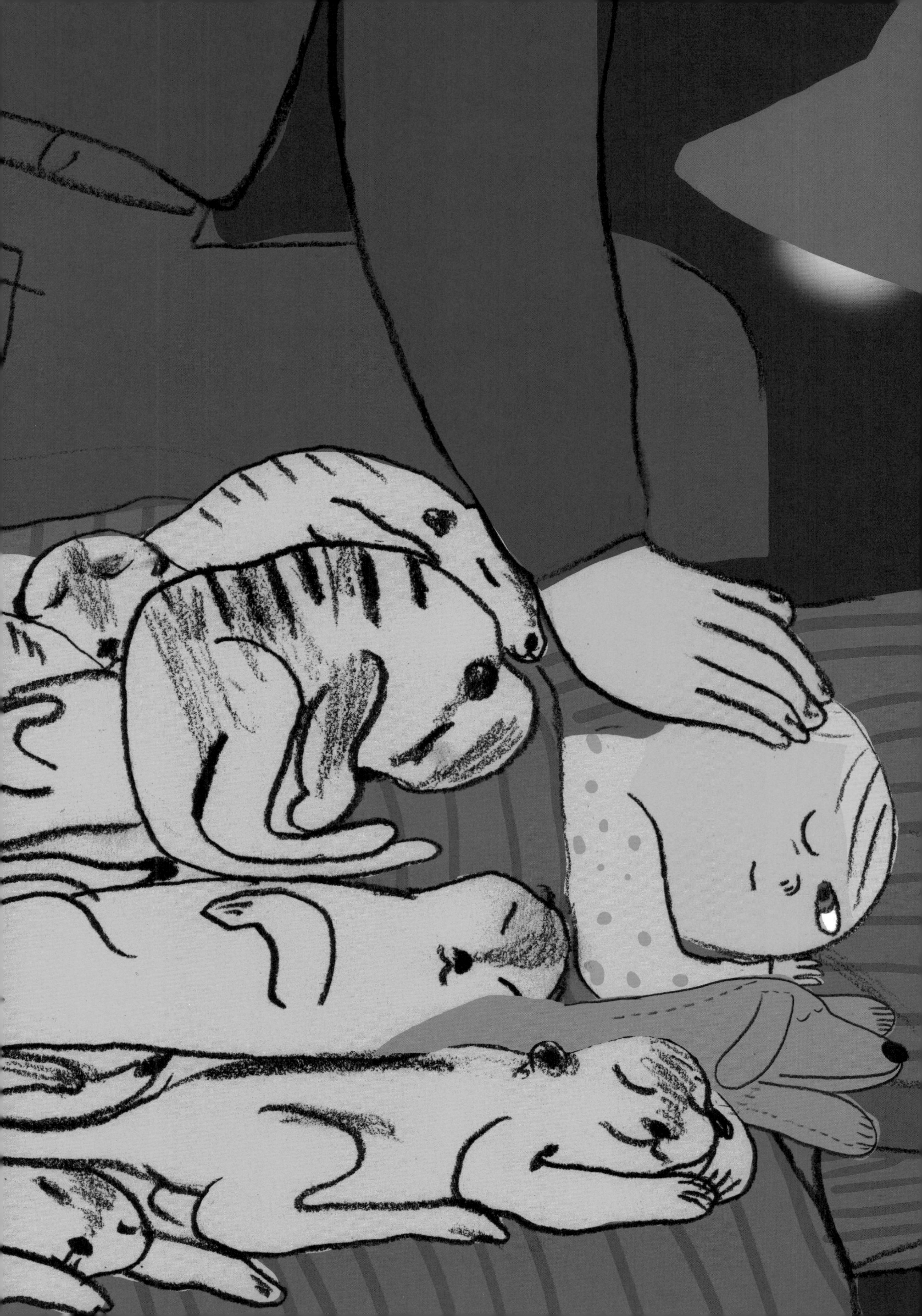

Mommy turns off the light.
The room is dark, but the stars
on the ceiling shine bright.

"And now you're a bird," whispers Mommy.
"A swift high up in the sky."

"You sleep as you fly,
through winter and summer,
over valley and hill,
over all those below you,
who sleep and are still."

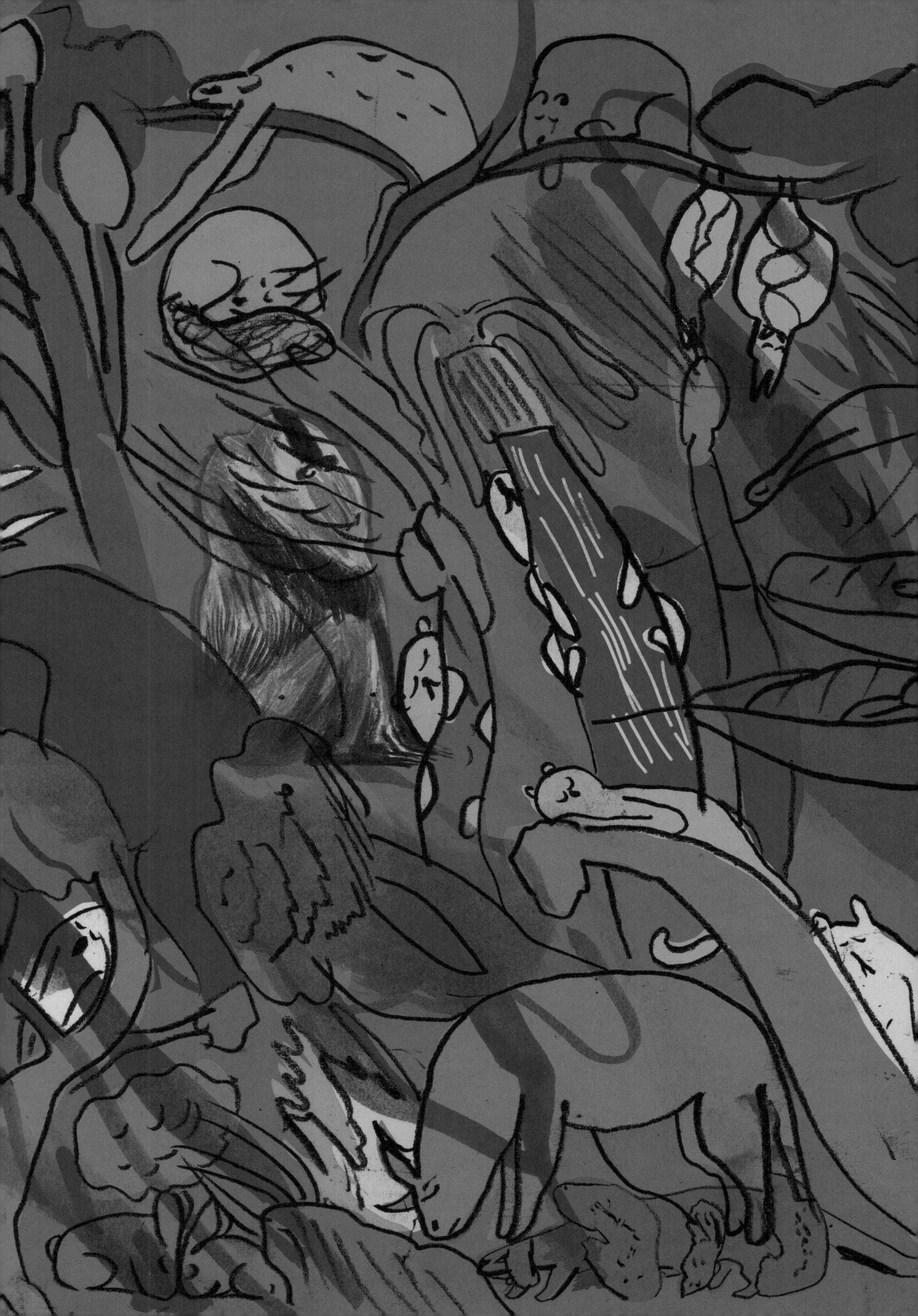

**This translation has been published with the financial support of NORLA. Enchanted Lion Books gratefully acknowledges this support.**

KJERSTI ANNESDATTER SKOMSVOLD is from Oslo, Norway. A versatile and prolific writer, Skomsvold writes fiction, poetry, and children's books. She made her literary debut in 2009 with the novel *The Faster I Walk, the Smaller I Am*, which was awarded the prestigious Tarjei Vesaas' First Book Prize and received numerous other accolades. It has been sold for translation into more than 25 languages. Skomsvold's second and third novels, *Monsterhuman* and *33*, enjoyed a similarly warm reception. In 2017, she published *The Child*, a critically acclaimed, highly personal novel on love and childbirth. In 2021, she published the picture book *Bedtime for Bo*, in collaboration with artist Mari Kanstad Johnsen.

**MARI KANSTAD JOHNSEN** is an awarded and acclaimed visual artist, children's book author, and illustrator. She has degrees from Oslo National Academy of the Arts and Konstfack University of Arts, Crafts and Design in Stockholm. In 2012, *Vivaldi*, which Kanstad Johnsen illustrated, was selected as one of *Flavorwire*'s "20 Most Beautiful Children's Books of All Time." In 2017, she was awarded a special mention at the international Bologna Ragazzi Awards. Mari Kanstad Johnsen has illustrated for several newspapers and magazines, including the *New York Times*.

**KARI DICKSON** was born in Edinburgh, Scotland, and grew up bilingually, as her mother is Norwegian and her grandparents could not speak English. She holds a B.A. in Scandinavian Studies and an M.A. in Translation. She has translated many books from Norwegian published by Enchanted Lion, including Batchelder-Award-winning *Brown*; *My Father's Arms Are a Boat*; *The Hole*; and *The Heartless Troll*.